Charlsie's Chuckle

by Clara Widess Berkus · photographs by Margaret Dodd
published by Woodbine House

The main characters in this story were played by the Heighes family, mother Wendy, father Raymond, little sister Riannon—and Randen, who portrays Charlsie. We deeply admire and respect this family who so freely gave their time, cooperation and humanity to this project. It was a privilege to come to know them and to be able to witness their exhilaration over their child's achievements, their occasional frustrations, and most of all their loving concern for their son, and the love and demonstration of affection he gave them in return.

Warm thanks to: B J Duke, Dave Fenske, Don Glasgow, Eric Reinhart and William Taylor for taking the parts of the Town Council; Christopher and Richard Dove, Molly Duke, Brittany Jordan, Shasta and Whitney Kellerhouse, J W Kirk II, Andrew and Jenny Jo Reinhart and Shannon Winters for participating in the party and parade scenes; Gary Allan, Pamela and Richard Armstrong, Marlene and Michael J Fine, Joyce Hart, Ellen Hunt, Eli Luria, Scott McClaine, Alex and Jacqui Meisel, Patricia Wormser and Suzanne Zavrian for assistance; the "Monday" writers who meet on Wednesday, for their support; and Anoli Perera for designing the masks.

Text copyright © 1992 by Clara Widess Berkus
Photographs copyright © 1992 by Margaret Dodd
Published in the USA by Woodbine House, Inc,
5615 Fishers Lane, Rockville, Maryland 20852
800-843-7323

Design by Margaret Dodd/Printed in Hong Kong

Library of Congress Cataloging-in-Publication Data
Berkus, Clara Widess.
    Charlsie's chuckle / by Clara Widess Berkus : photographs by Margaret Dodd.
        p.   cm.
    Summary: Charlsie, a young boy with Down's syndrome, has an infectious chuckle that helps the members of the Town Council stop arguing long enough to solve some serious problems.
    ISBN 0-933149-50-6 : $14.95
    [1. Down's syndrome—Fiction.   2. Mentally handicapped—Fiction.
3. Laughter—Fiction.]   I. Dodd, Margaret, ill.   II. Title.
PZ7.B45322Ch   1992   [Fic]—dc20   91-46655   CIP   AC

10 9 8 7 6 5 4 3 2 1

To Barry and Gail,
who believed
from the start.

Not too far from your house, there lives a boy who has the happiest, most catching chuckle that ever was.

Yet, when he was born, nobody celebrated with balloons or parties. For Charlsie looked different from other babies. His doctor used the words *Down syndrome* and said that Charlsie would be slower to learn than other children.

But before long, when something made Charlsie happy, his eyes would brighten, his nose would wrinkle, and a chuckle would come from his throat like no sound anyone had ever heard before. It was like music blown by the wind. Like birds welcoming the sun with a song.

No one could hear that chuckle without feeling a little happier. Until they thought about how sad it was that Charlsie had been born different.

4

Many things made Charlsie chuckle.
A butterfly winging by his window. His mother
smiling at him in the morning. His father tossing
him high.

His chuckle held even more joy on the days
he learned to do something all by himself.

Everyone in Charlsie's family felt happier
with each new thing Charlsie learned, even though
it took him longer than anyone else to learn it.
But they wanted more for him. And the sad look
never quite left his mother's eyes.

Then bad times came to the town where Charlsie lived. The spring rains didn't fall. The earth dried. People who had never gone hungry before had nothing to eat. And people who had always lived in nice houses had to sleep in the park.

The members of the Town Council tried to decide what to do. They sat at a long table in the Town Hall from morning till night, trying.

They grew weary. Everyone wanted to help but no one could agree with anyone else on what to do.

By the thirtieth day, they were shouting at each other.

Now it so happened that Charlsie's seventh birthday fell on the day that the Council was meeting for the thirtieth time. And to celebrate Charlsie's birthday, Charlsie's mother and little sister gave him a party. And his father gave him a bright blue bicycle with training wheels.

Charlsie chuckled and chuckled as he rode the new bicycle all over the yard. His friends at the party cheered to see how well Charlsie was riding.

When his friends had gone, Charlsie decided to take a longer ride on his bicycle.

He waved goodbye to his mother, watching from the porch steps. She would never stop watching, Charlsie knew, until her special boy was safely home.

Out of his yard and down the road Charlsie went.
The new bicycle pedaled so easily, he kept on going.
Before Charlsie knew it, he was passing the Town Hall
where the Council was meeting for the thirtieth time.

Charlsie had never heard anything like
the shouting that came from the window above.
He stopped pedaling to listen.

At that moment, someone called someone else a penny pincher for not using the town money to feed the hungry and find houses for people who had nowhere to live.

A woman in an angry voice called someone an unbending stickler for not letting the homeless pitch tents in the park.

A man shouted that the woman had bees in her bonnet not to see the problems a park full of campers would lead to.

Another man called someone a stubborn mule for refusing to lower the cost of electricity and gas for all who couldn't afford to pay for them.

Then many voices shouted that someone was a blockhead for not solving the town's problems long ago.

Charlsie tried to picture what a penny pincher looked like. Or a stickler who couldn't bend. Or a woman with bees in her bonnet. Or a man like a mule. Or a blockhead.

Charlsie's mother had told him never to go anywhere he wasn't invited. And his father had warned him that he could get into trouble if he did. But Charlsie was so curious that he left his bicycle near the window and climbed the steps of the Town Hall.

Everyone Charlsie passed looked at him as if he might be going where he didn't belong. But no one did anything about it. So he kept on walking as if he was on serious business. He tried not to chuckle as he thought of the funny looking people he was going to see.

The shouting grew louder as he walked down the corridor. And loudest behind a door with big gold letters.

16

Since Charlsie had been told never to enter a room before knocking, he tapped on the door very politely. When no one answered, he opened the door and looked in.

But there were only four ordinary looking men and one ordinary looking woman at a long table.

No one was pinching pennies. No one looked like a stickler. No one had bees in her bonnet. There was no mule. And no blockhead.

The people at the table looked so ordinary that it seemed funnier and funnier that they should spend so much time pounding on the table and shouting at each other.

Charlsie began to chuckle. His chuckle rang out deeper than the deepest shout in the room and higher than the voice of the woman who looked too nice to be so angry.

Everyone at the table looked around in surprise.
And suddenly Charlsie's chuckle was the only sound that
could be heard in the Council Chamber.

The mouths of all the people at the table dropped
open at the same time.

Slowly, the grim look left the eyes of one.
The eyebrows of another uncreased. Everyone
stopped glaring.

Then the man at the head of the table
let out a deep guffaw.

A sound that hadn't been heard in the Council
Chamber for thirty days shook the rafters.

Some laughs were high, some low, and some squeaky
from being rusty so long. The laughs went on and on
as if laughter felt so good, no one wanted to stop.

Charlsie stopped chuckling
because he couldn't see anything
funny now about the people
sitting around the table.

"Excuse me, please, for
interrupting your meeting,"
he said in his most grownup
voice. With that, he walked from
the room, down the corridor
and out of the Town Hall.

He was about to leave when the woman's voice rose above all the others.

"And to think that we might still be arguing if that boy hadn't come into the Council Chamber!" she said. "Do you suppose any other town ever owed so much to a small boy's chuckle?"

Charlsie was about to pedal off when he heard excited voices from above.

Someone was talking about starting a job training center. Another about letting tents go up in the park. Another about lowering the cost of gas and electricity for those who couldn't afford to pay.

The man with the deep voice thanked everyone for being so cooperative. Then everyone, speaking at once, said that they had known all along what a fine Mayor he was.

Charlsie heard the words but puzzled about what they meant.

23

A warm feeling crept into Charlsie's stomach and spread up into his throat and head.

He pedaled off as fast as he could, trying to hold on to the good feeling until he got home.

Charlsie's mother gave him a big hug, glad that her
very special boy was safely home. But the sad look still lay
in her eyes, the look that never quite seemed to go away.

Charlsie wanted to tell her that she didn't have to be sad anymore. That something had happened that made everything all right. But he didn't know how to say it.

He sat on his swing and pushed hard. He swung higher and higher. Higher than he had ever dared swing before.

The chuckle that came from his throat was like the music of a heavenly choir.

His mother, listening, knew that Charlsie was trying to tell her something. But she couldn't tell what it was. Her heart full of love, she chuckled softly with Charlsie. But with a sob in her throat because she wanted so much to understand.

Soon, the story of what had happened in the Council
Chamber spread all over town. A reporter was sent out
to find the boy who had helped the town so much.
    And the very next day, there was Charlsie's picture
on the front page of the morning newspaper.

The Mayor declared a special Chuckling Charlsie Day.
With a parade and balloons.
And with Charlsie riding at the head of the parade.

When Charlsie waved to his mother, he chuckled
deeper and gladder than he had ever chuckled
before. Because the sad look was gone from her eyes.

And all the people watching the parade chuckled
along with Charlsie as he rode by.

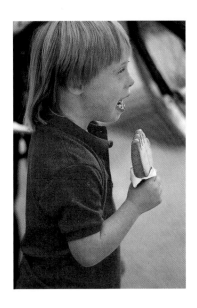

Down syndrome is a chromosomal disorder present at birth, characterized by some degree of mental retardation, certain physical characteristics, and difficulties in speech and language. The exact cause and prevention are currently unknown. Prompt treatment of medical problems that may arise and educational interventions are extremely important in minimizing the effect of Down syndrome on a person's life.

The incidence of Down syndrome is approximately one in every thousand births, with over one quarter of a million people in the United States affected. It is possible for a woman of any age to bear a child with Down syndrome. Although the likelihood increases with maternal age, women under thirty-five give birth to more than eighty percent of these babies.

Children with Down syndrome, like all children, display wide variation in physical development, mental abilities and behavior. They need to be treated with dignity and accorded the same rights as other children. Loving family support, inclusive educational, social, recreational and work opportunities, along with reasonable expectations of achievement, all contribute to helping people with Down syndrome develop their potential and move towards independence.

— Michal C Clark, PhD
President, National Down
Syndrome Congress